Ge ral   F. ORM

KU-639-922

starchasers
the jungle planet

WITHDRAWN

by

dauid orme

illustrated by
jorge mongioui

Ransom

bury College
Woodbury LRC

starchasers

The Jungle Planet
by David Orme

Illustrated by Jorge Mongiovi

Published by Ransom Publishing Ltd.
51 Southgate Street, Winchester, Hants. SO23 9EH, UK

www.ransom.co.uk

ISBN   978 184167 768 2

First published in 2009

Copyright © 2009 Ransom Publishing Ltd.
Illustrations copyright © 2009 Jorge Mongiovi

A CIP catalogue record of this book is available from the British Library.

The rights of David Orme to be identified as the author and of Jorge Mongiovi to be identified as the illustrator of this Work have been asserted by them in accordance with sections 77 and 78 of the Copyright, Design and Patents Act 1988.

dauid orme

has written too many books to count, ranging from poetry to non-fiction.

When he is not writing he travels around the UK, giving performances and running writing workshops.

David is a huge science fiction fan and has the biggest collection of science fiction magazines that the Starchasers have ever seen.

Bury College
LRC

C. Chartres
July 12
6.00 .

Bury College
Woodbury LRC

Millennium

Woodbury Centre

00269217

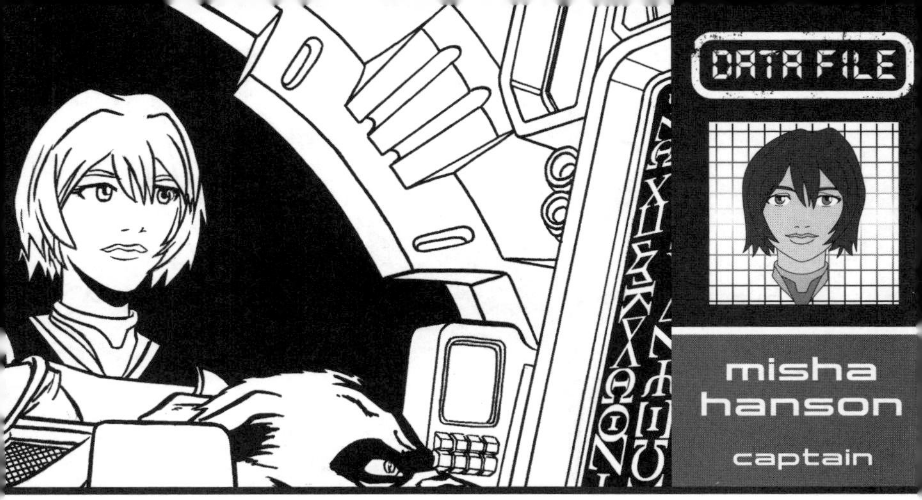
DATA FILE
misha
hanson
captain

- Owner of the *Lightspinner*.
- When her rich father died, Misha could have lived in luxury – but that was much too boring.
- She spent all the money on the *Lightspinner* – and a life of adventure!
- Misha is the boss – but she doesn't always get her own way.

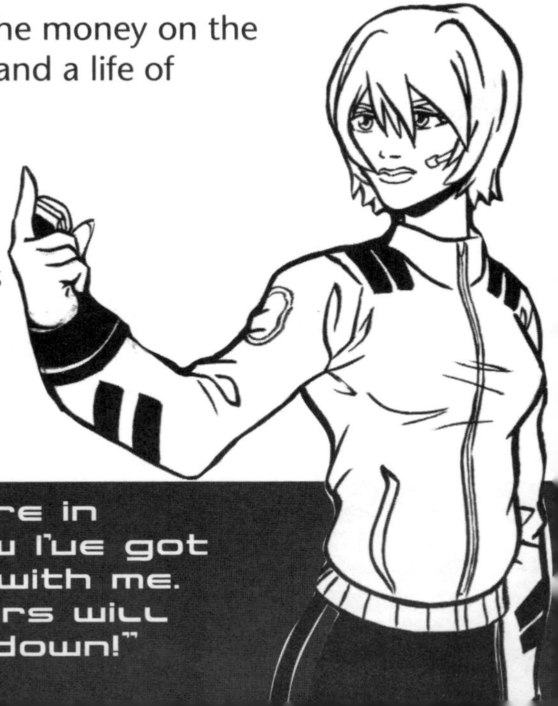

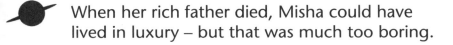

"Whenever we're in trouble, I know I've got a great team with me. The Starchasers will never let me down!"

DATA FILE

suma

science officer

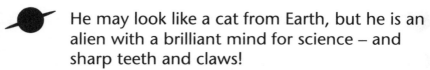

- He may look like a cat from Earth, but he is an alien with a brilliant mind for science – and sharp teeth and claws!

- Probably the smartest cat in space. Finn and Misha don't need to tell him that – he knows!

- Suma's not always easy to get on with. Take care – he makes a dangerous enemy!

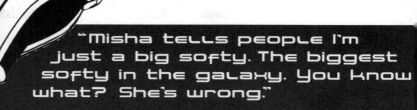

"Misha tells people I'm just a big softy. The biggest softy in the galaxy. You know what? She's wrong."

DATA FILE

finn 2021

pilot

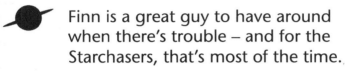 Finn is a great guy to have around when there's trouble – and for the Starchasers, that's most of the time.

Probably the best pilot Planet Earth has ever produced – though Misha and Suma don't tell him that, of course!

Finn is great for getting the Starchasers out of (and sometimes in to) trouble! If only he didn't love gadgets so much …

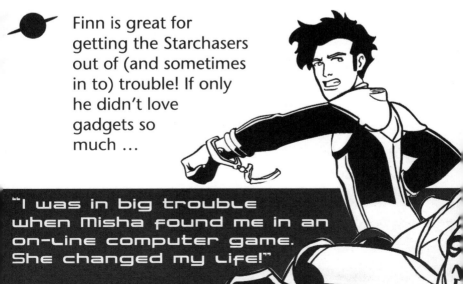

"I was in big trouble when Misha found me in an on-line computer game. She changed my life!"

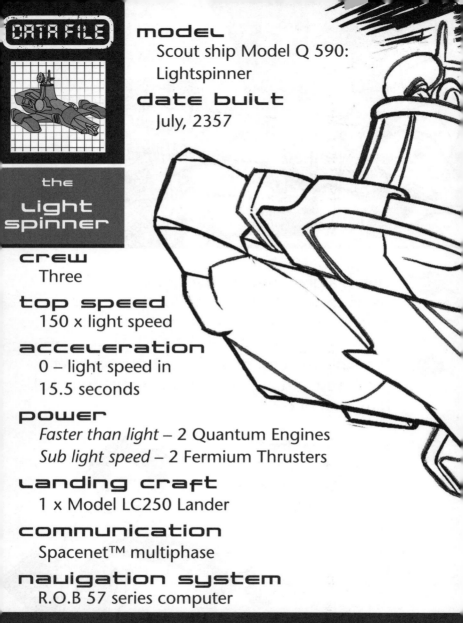

DATA FILE

model
Scout ship Model Q 590:
Lightspinner

date built
July, 2357

the
**Light
spinner**

crew
Three

top speed
150 x light speed

acceleration
0 – light speed in
15.5 seconds

power
Faster than light – 2 Quantum Engines
Sub light speed – 2 Fermium Thrusters

landing craft
1 x Model LC250 Lander

communication
Spacenet™ multiphase

navigation system
R.O.B 57 series computer

*"THE TOP-OF-THE-RANGE SOUND
SYSTEM WILL BLOW YOUR MIND!"*
SPACE SOUNDS   APRIL 2357

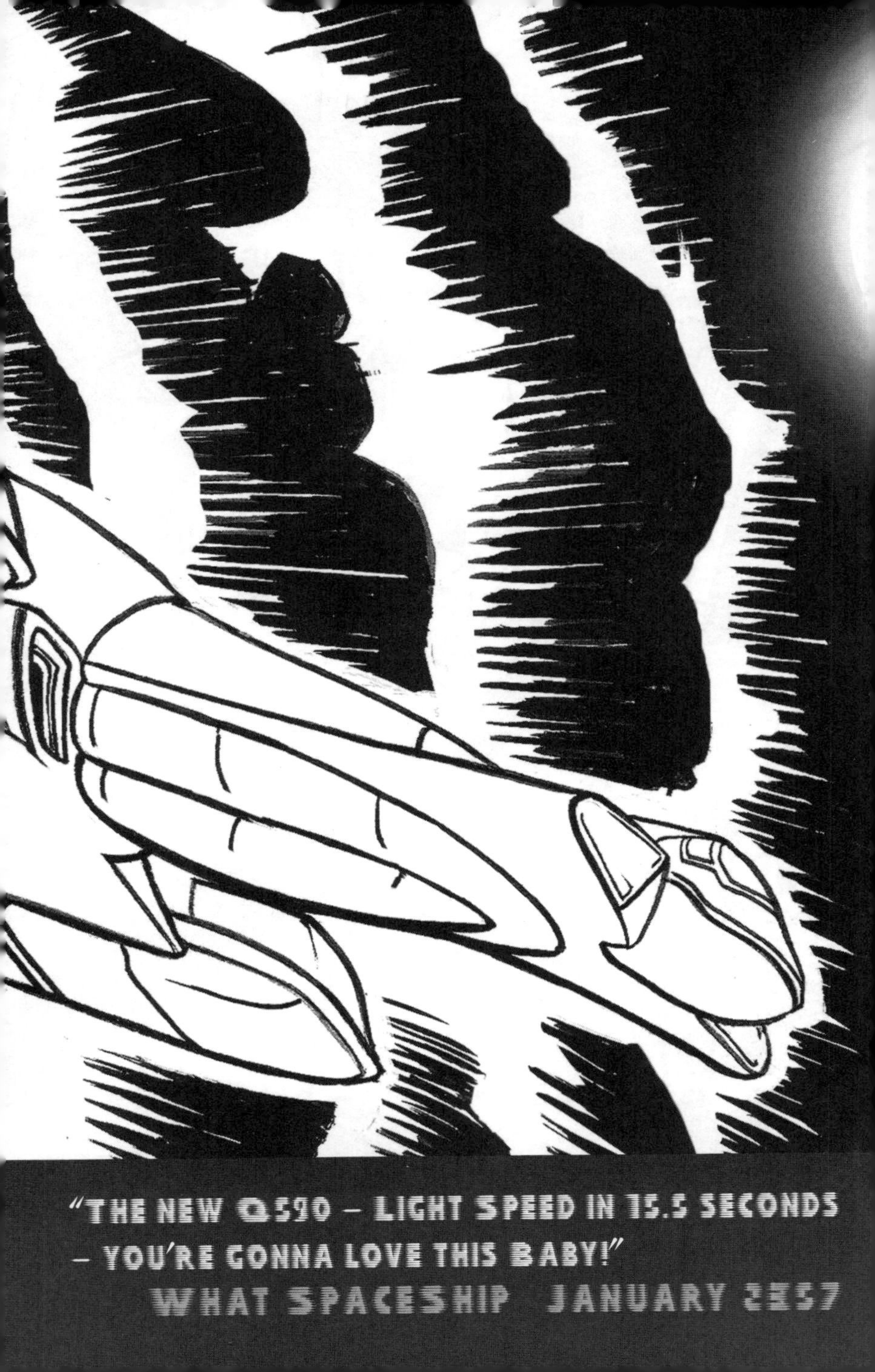

"THE NEW Q590 – LIGHT SPEED IN 15.5 SECONDS – YOU'RE GONNA LOVE THIS BABY!"

WHAT SPACESHIP JANUARY 2357

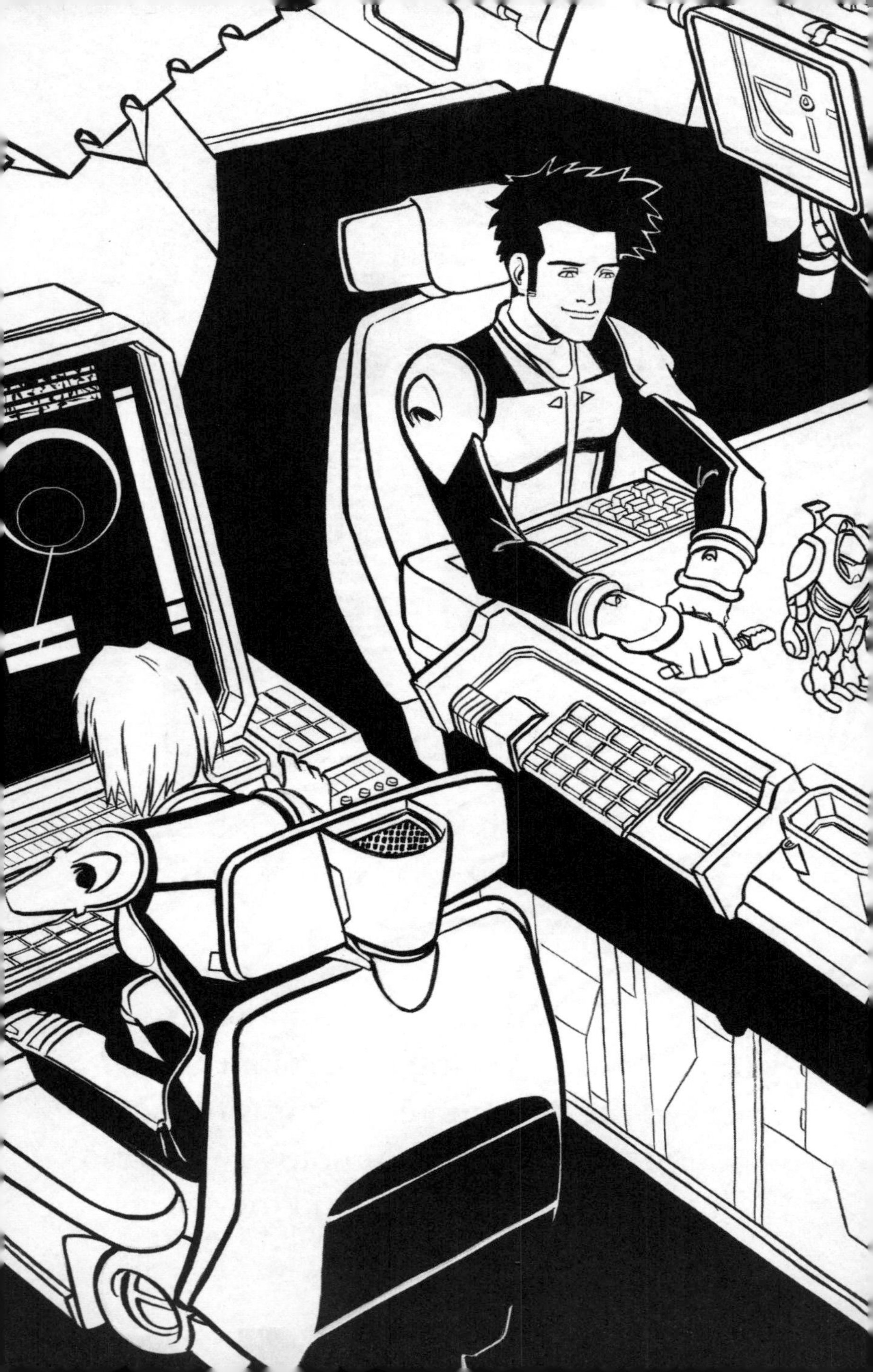

a new mission

'So what do we do now?'

The Starchasers hadn't had a job for over three weeks. At first, they were glad of the break. Suma worked in his laboratory on a secret project. Finn had some new gadgets to play with. Misha spent the time checking out their spaceship, the Lightspinner. She checked the quantum engine was running smoothly, and updated the software that ran Rob, the ship's computer. And they all waited for the spacephone to ring with the offer of a well-paid job. But the call didn't come.

'So what do we do now?' Finn said again. This time, Suma came up with something.

'I have an idea. It's risky, but it might just work out.'

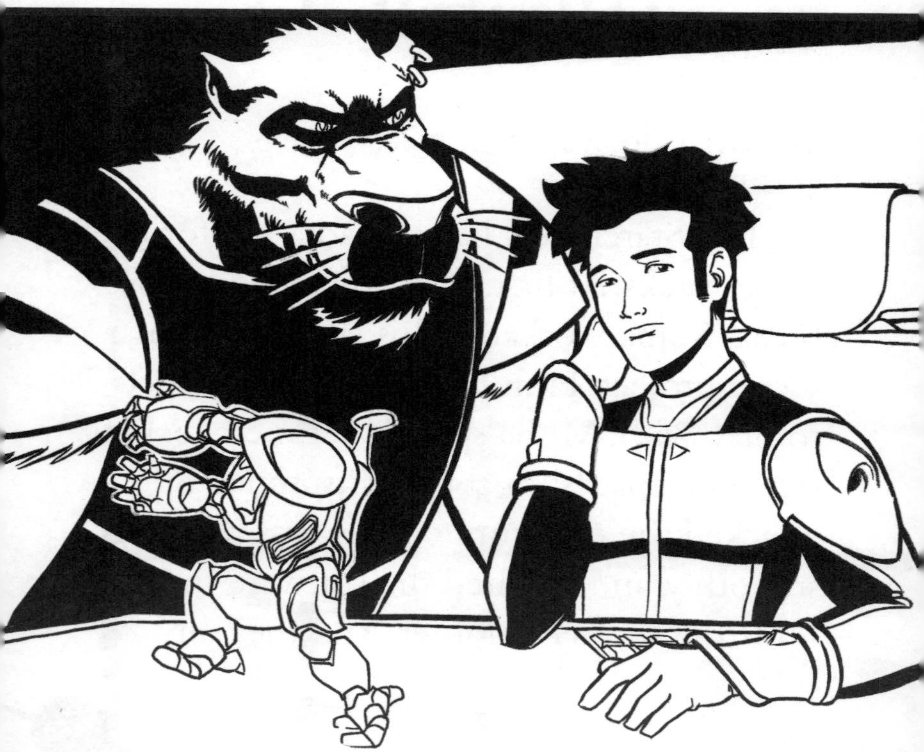

'Oh no, not another one of your crazy missions!' groaned Finn. 'Remember the planet with those creatures that looked like rocks? Remember what happened when I sat on one? I needed a soft cushion to sit on for a whole week!'

'As I was saying,' Suma went on, 'I have an idea. You know that nebula, out past Rigel? There were some interesting readings on the scanner when we passed it. What do you think?'

'You want me to navigate through a nebula? You know how dangerous they are!' grumbled Finn.

'How dangerous they *used to be*. Have you uploaded that new software, Misha? That will make all the difference. No one has explored a nebula before. There could be stuff there that will make all our fortunes! Are you two up for it?'

They were up for it. That evening, the Lightspinner blasted out of Earth's orbit. When it was a safe distance away, Finn powered up the Q-engine.

A rainbow ring appeared in front of the ship – the entrance to the wormhole. Finn hit full power. Mission on!

into the nebula

The new navigation software was brilliant.

Nebulas were clouds of dust in space. They could be huge, many light–years across, with stars and planets inside. Most people thought it was too dangerous to go into a nebula. It was hard for the computer to fix on a target because of the dust.

This meant that when you came out of the wormhole you might end up anywhere – even inside a sun!

The Lightspinner dropped into normal space outside the nebula. Suma checked the position of the sun he was interested in.

'O.K., Finn. Let's go!'

Keeping his fingers crossed, Finn powered up the engine. Seconds later, the stars vanished.

Almost instantly they appeared again – but they looked very different. It was like being in mist. All around, the spacedust shone with light from stars that glowed deep in the nebula: red dwarf stars, yellow stars like Earth's own Sun, and huge blue-coloured giants, dangerous to go near.

BUILT

Most of the stars would have planets, and none of these had been explored!

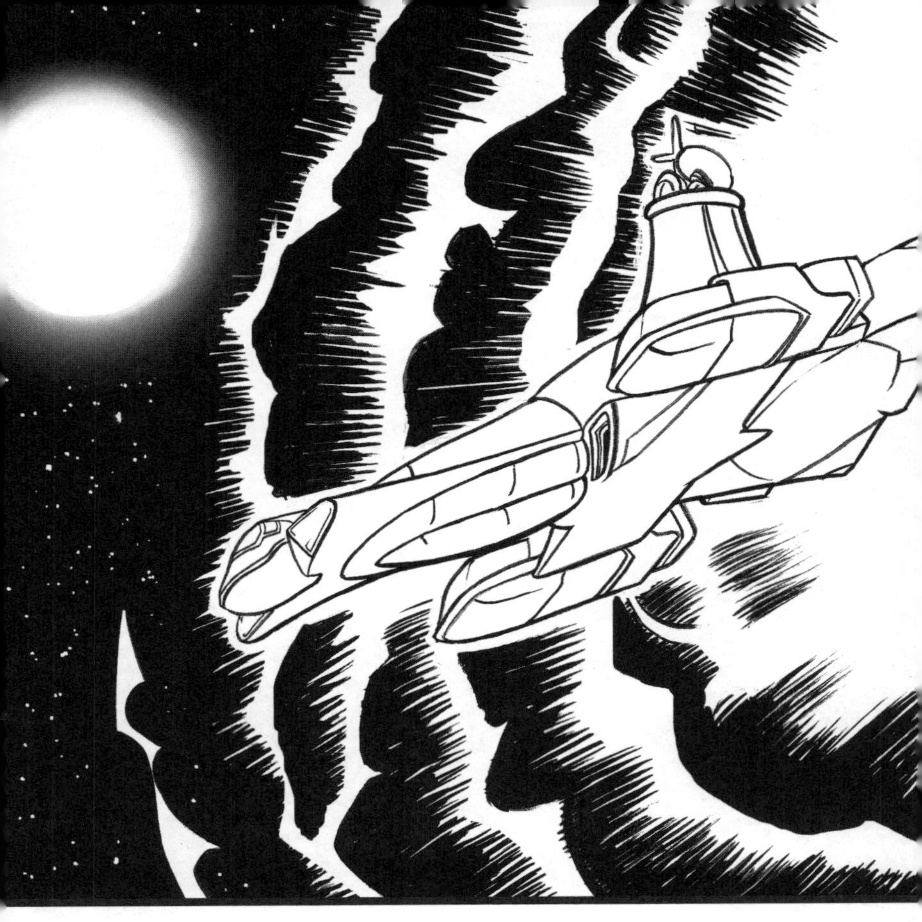

'Perfect!' said Finn. 'That star you were aiming at is right ahead!'

The ship's scanners started working. They were looking for planets that might have life – not too near and not too far from the sun.

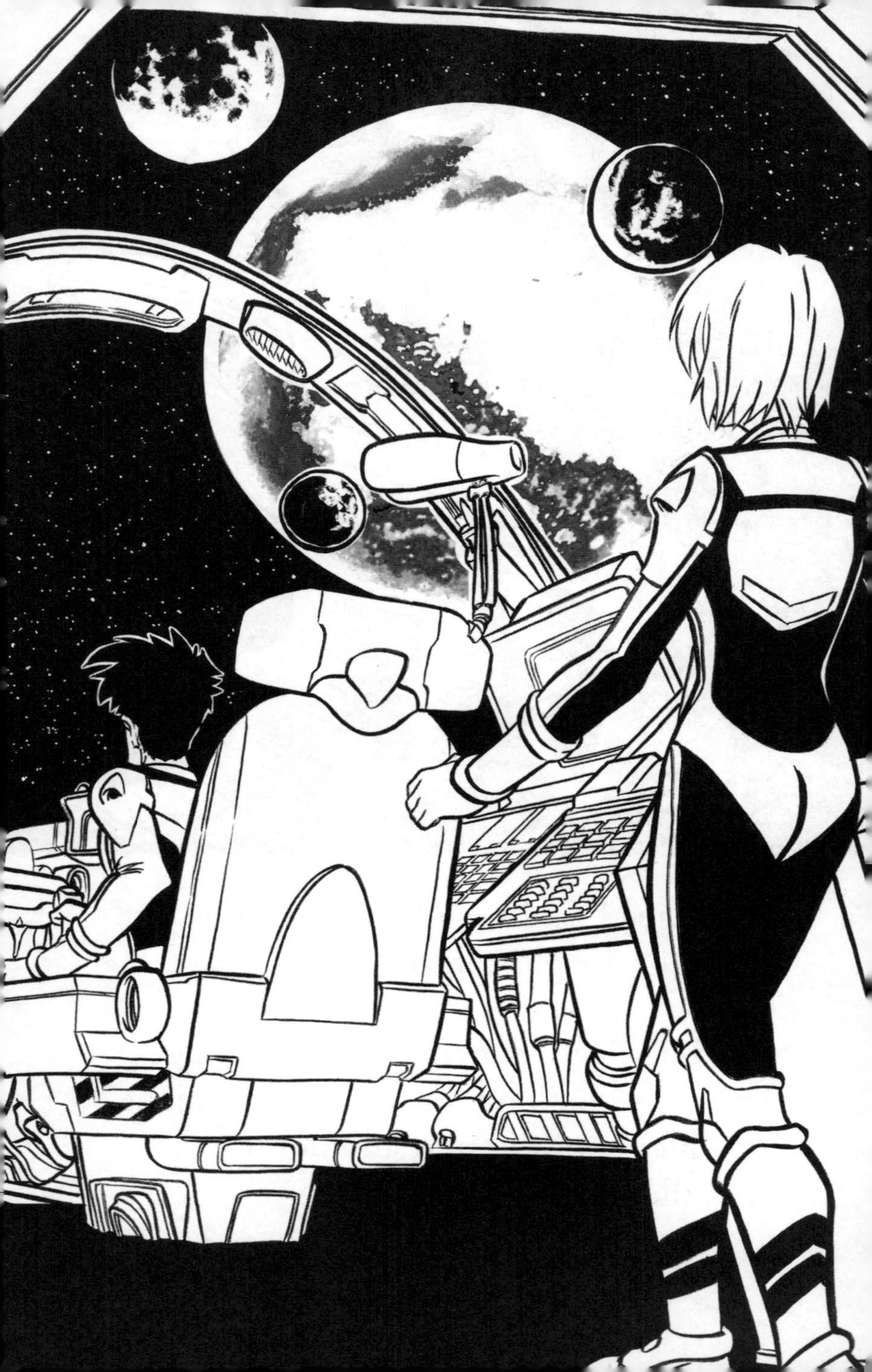

'Got one. Let's check it out.'

Finn headed slowly towards the new planet. Most of the nebula dust in that part of space had been sucked into the sun, but he didn't want to take chances. Even a tiny speck of dust could damage a spaceship if you were travelling at full speed.

The planet looked perfect. White clouds, blue seas – it could have been another Earth.

'Three moons,' said Misha. 'We'll set up our base on the biggest one.'

The Starchasers never landed on an unknown planet straight away. Explorers who tried it sometimes ended up dead!

junGLe
pLanet

First, Suma ran a check for intelligent life. The number one rule for exploring space – if you find intelligent creatures, get out of there quick. They had to be left alone to develop in their own way. But intelligent life was rare in the galaxy.

'No sign of any buildings, and no radio or TV signals,' said Misha. 'I think we're O.K. But landing isn't going to be easy!'

The planet was the usual mix of oceans and continents. And apart from the frozen north and south poles, everything was covered with thick jungle.

Misha moved the scanner across the planet.

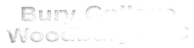
Bury College
Wood...

'Look,' she said. 'Bare patches, scattered here and there. Looks like places where trees have come down in a storm.'

'Suma and I'll take the lander down and have a look around,' Finn said. 'We'll look for one of those bare places once we're there.'

A few hours later, Finn and Suma were skimming over the jungle.

'Over there!' said Suma. 'One of these clear spots!'

Finn nodded and aimed the lander at the clear space. Misha was right. A whole chunk of the jungle had been knocked flat in a storm.

Carefully, carefully, he took the lander down, watching all the time for rocks that

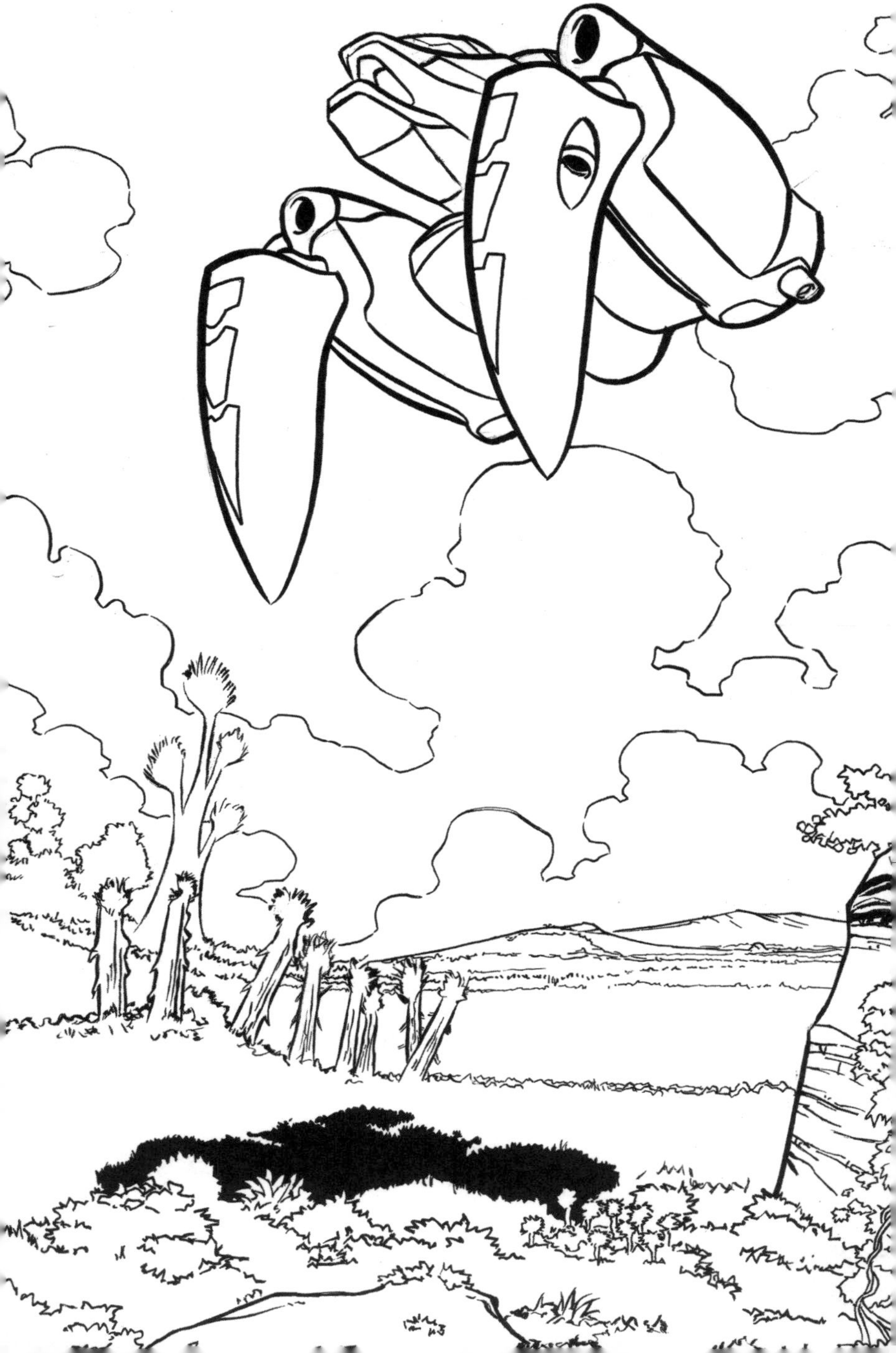

could tip it over. At last he cut the engines.

'Made it!'

Suma just nodded. Finn had done a brilliant job.

'What now?' asked Finn.

'We wait. Days and nights are short on this planet. In thirty Earth minutes it will be dark. We'll get some sleep, then have a look outside. I've checked the air. It's O.K. to breathe, but make sure you wear the air filter at all times. There's bound to be some crazy bugs on this planet.'

Night came, but it wasn't dark, like on Earth. The night was lit up with a white glow, which made it impossible to see the stars. Two moons were in the sky; soon the third moon, with Misha and the Lightspinner on it, would be up as well.

The hours passed, and daylight came. Suma opened the airlock. The first thing you notice on a new planet is the smell – it's never like anything you've ever met before.

Then there's the noise. And this planet had noise – and plenty of it: screaming, whistling, and distant roars like the sound of fighting dinosaurs. There was lots of life – but was it friendly?

trapped!

Suma got ready to explore.

'I'm just heading out to collect some samples. I'll be a little while. I'll keep in touch. Keep alert.'

Finn nodded. Suma was best left alone on jobs like this. Finn would only get in the way. If Suma hit trouble, his cat-like body could move faster than most species in the galaxy.

Finn settled back in the pilot's seat. It was all very well for Suma to say 'keep alert' but it was boring, just sitting there.

What could go wrong?

He reached for a bag he had brought with him. Inside was his virtual game helmet. Might as well try and finish his game of 'Toxic Alien 3 – The Final Slobber' while he was waiting.

An hour later he was still playing. The toxic aliens had broken out and were heading for the castle Finn was trying to defend. His weapons were running out. One drip of their slobber and it was 'Game Over' for Finn!

He was really into the game, and he hadn't heard the loud buzz from the pilot's desk. At last he heard it.

He pulled of the helmet and switched on the radio. It was Misha.

'Guys! Is anyone down there? What's going on?'

Finn realised that he hadn't done a very good job of keeping alert!

'Hi Misha! Er – all fine here!'

'All fine? So why can't I see you on the ground viewer? You've disappeared! All I can see is green jungle!'

Finn looked around and realised that things had gone very dark. He tried to open the airlock door. At first it wouldn't open, but at last he managed to force it.

The lander was completely covered with green creepers! Finn slammed the door shut.

'Misha, looks like we have a small plant problem here. Don't worry, I'll get it sorted.'

'Finn, how could you let that happen. You haven't been playing that game again … ?'

'Misha, I'll get back to you.'

Finn flicked off the radio and collected some tools from the lander's tool box. Unless he got the plants clear, he was in big trouble – they all were.

The door wouldn't open again. With an effort he forced his way out and started hacking at the plants.

They were like thick, rubbery creepers, and they grew – fast. As he cut through one bit, a bit he had already chopped started growing again. It was a race – and one he was losing!

Just then Suma arrived.

'What on Earth's going on here?'

'We're not on Earth, Suma. I only wish we were!'

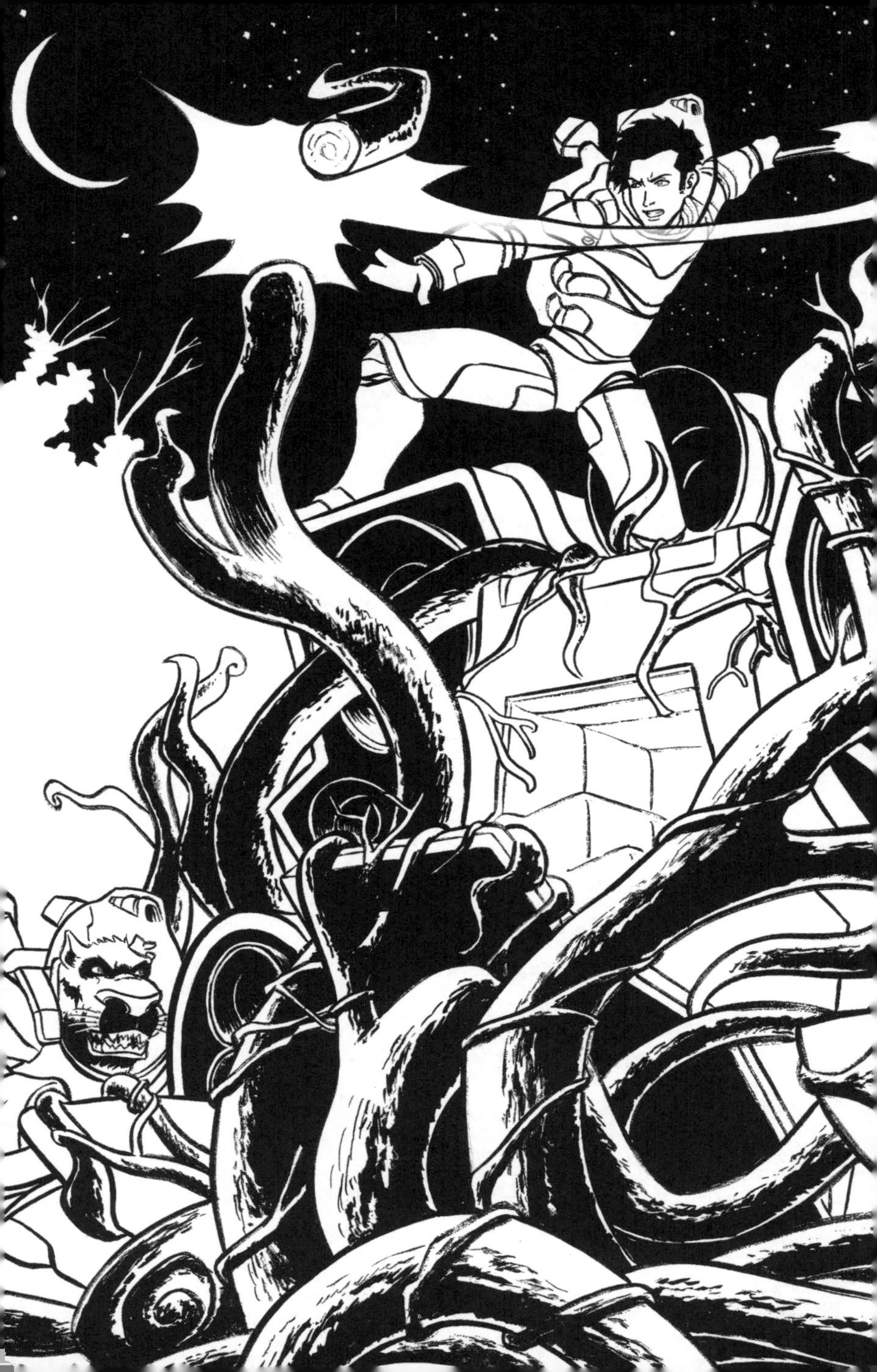

finn has
an idea

There was only one thing for it. Misha would have to bring the Lightspinner down and help. Misha was O.K. as a pilot, but she wasn't as good as Finn.

It was a big ask.

Finn thought of something that might get him back in favour.

'I've got an idea. Patch me in to Rob. I'll use the V-helmet to fly the Lightspinner.'

It was a great idea. Misha was relieved. She wouldn't have to land the big spaceship after all!

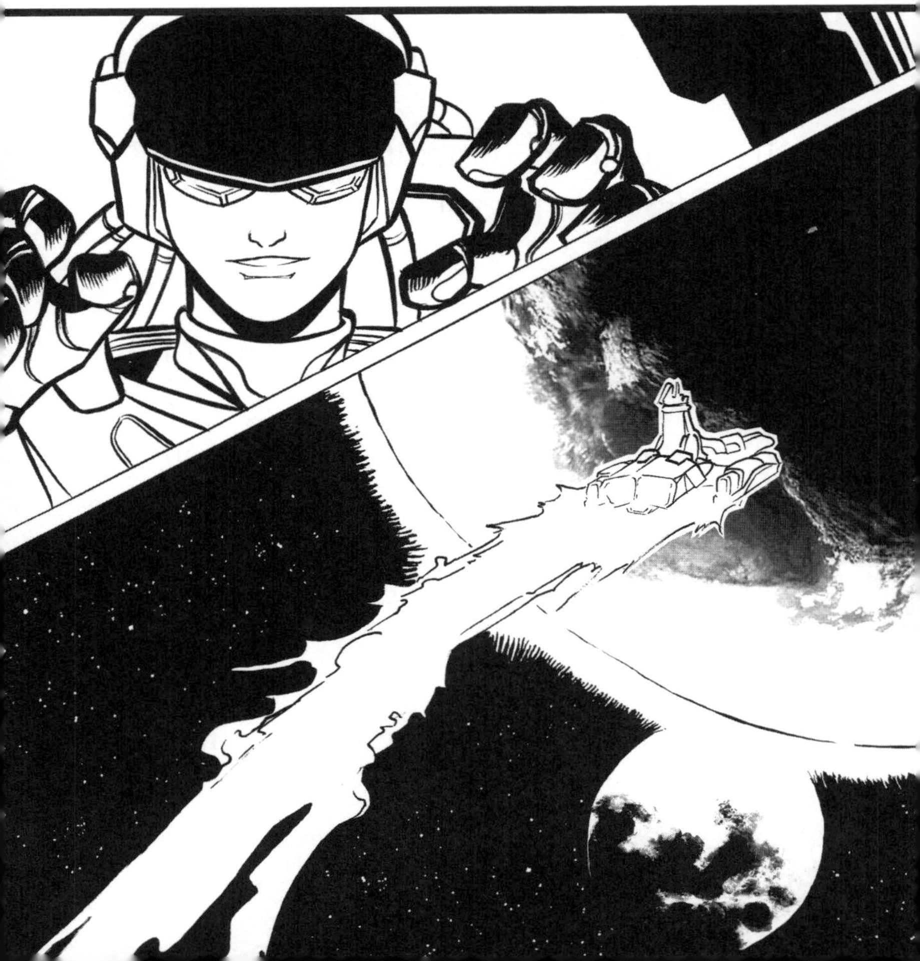

Using the virtual helmet, it was just like being on board the Lightspinner. Expertly, Finn started piloting the spaceship down through the clouds. All Misha had to do was watch.

There was one big problem. The bare patch on the planet had gone! Somehow, they were going to have to make a space for the Lightspinner to land.

'It's going to be difficult,' Finn had told Suma. 'These creepers are almost impossible to cut.'

'Should be O.K. The creepers only grow where the ground was bare. The rest of the jungle is made of trees, just like Earth ones. I can cut those, no problem.'

There was a problem, though. The airlock door was covered with creepers again!

At last they forced it open, and Suma went off with a laser saw.

This was just the thing to get some trees cleared so Finn could put down the Lightspinner's long landing legs. This way, the spaceship itself would stay above the trees.

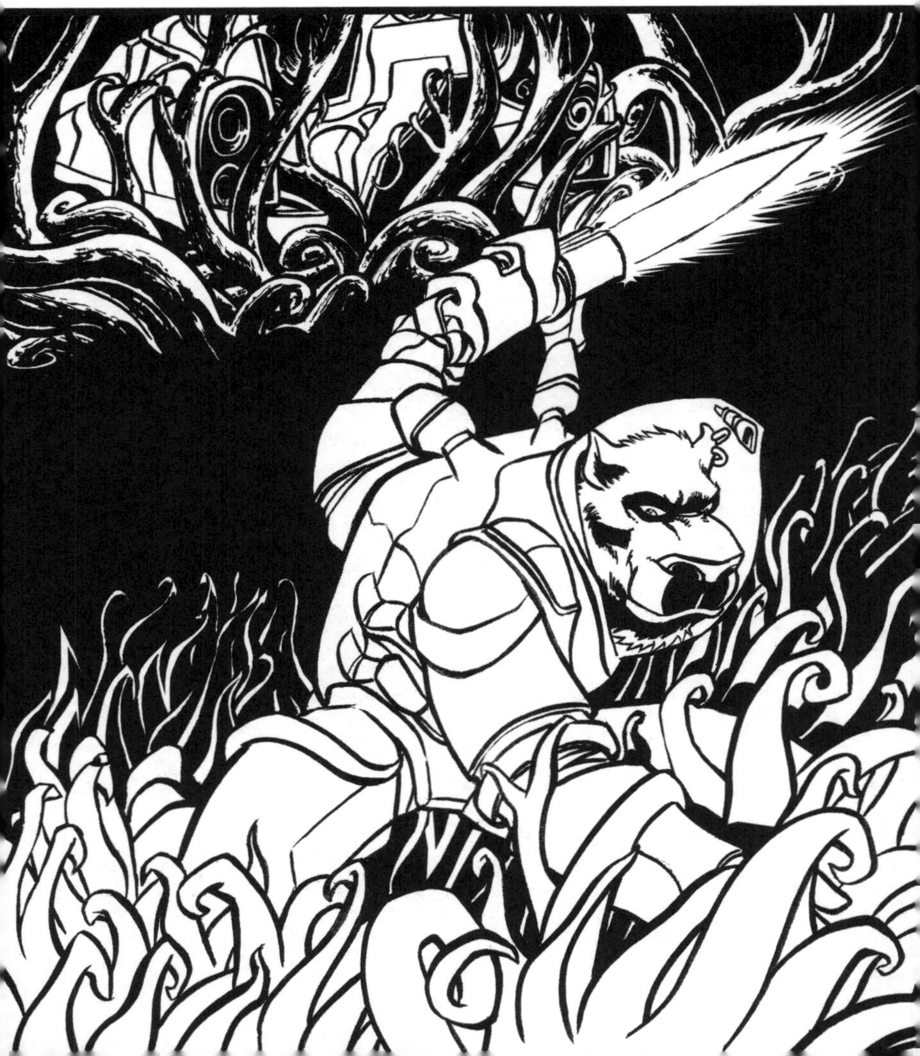

When Suma got back to the lander, there were even more of the rubbery creepers winding round it.

They knew that, even with Misha's help, it would be impossible to cut it free. Losing the lander would be a big and expensive blow to the Starchasers.

Suma set to work cutting back the creepers that covered the airlock door again.

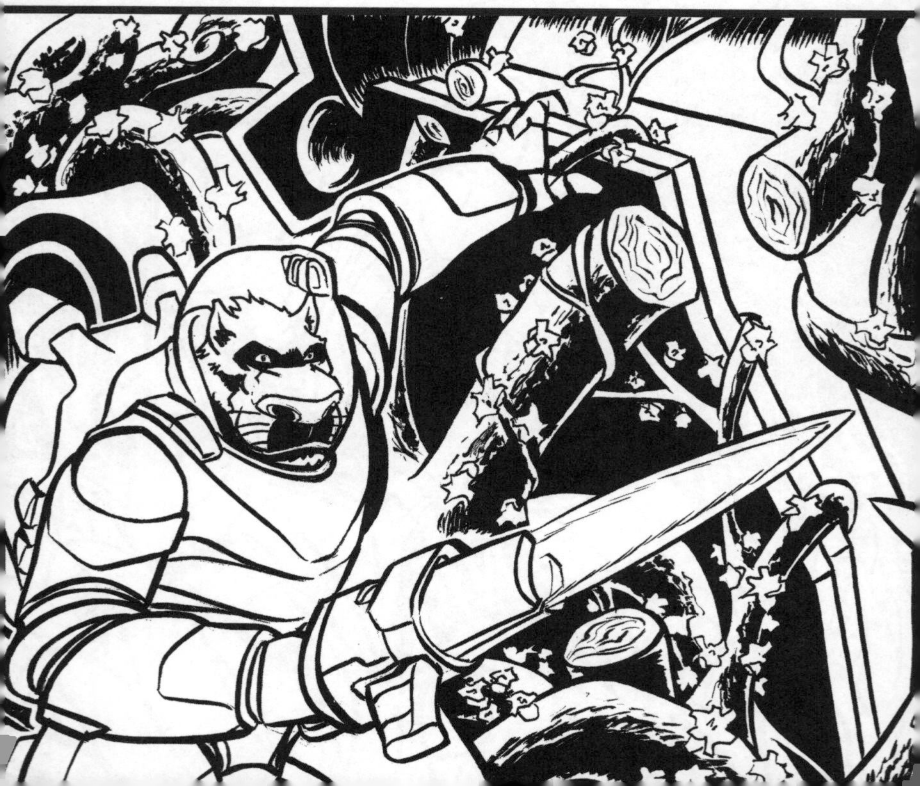

The laser saw was too dangerous to use this close to the lander. Suma just had to hack it away.

Then he noticed that buds were forming on the ends of the creeper. As he watched, the buds opened and bright red flowers appeared.

Suma was just admiring them when he heard a buzzing sound. Insects, the same colour as the flowers, were heading this

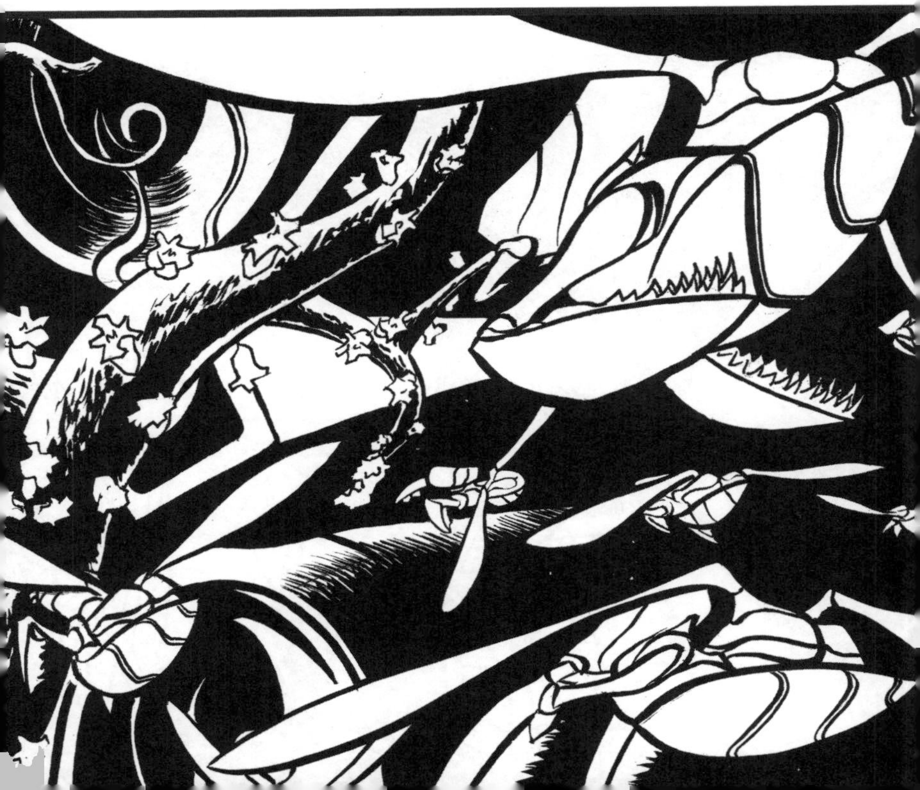

way! Insects could sting. He opened the airlock door just in time and slipped inside the lander.

He needn't have worried. The insects weren't after him. It was the flowers they wanted!

Suma and Finn watched as they buzzed around, gathering purple pollen.

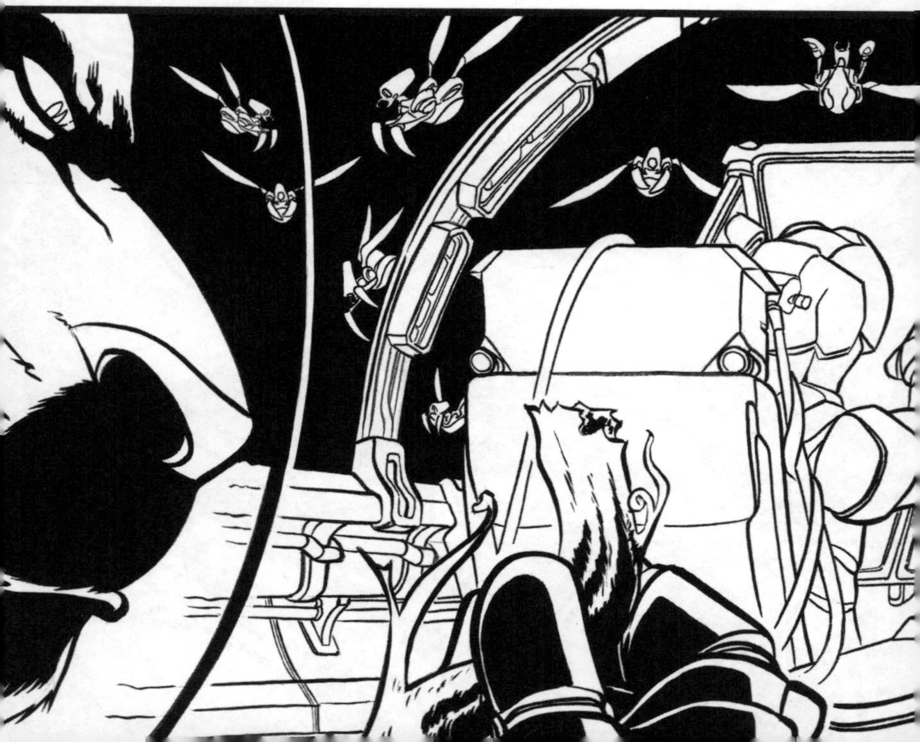

'These plants are amazing!' Suma said. 'There's nothing in the galaxy to touch them for growing speed!'

Suma seemed really excited about the plants. Finn couldn't care less about them. He just wanted to get out of the jungle and back into space.

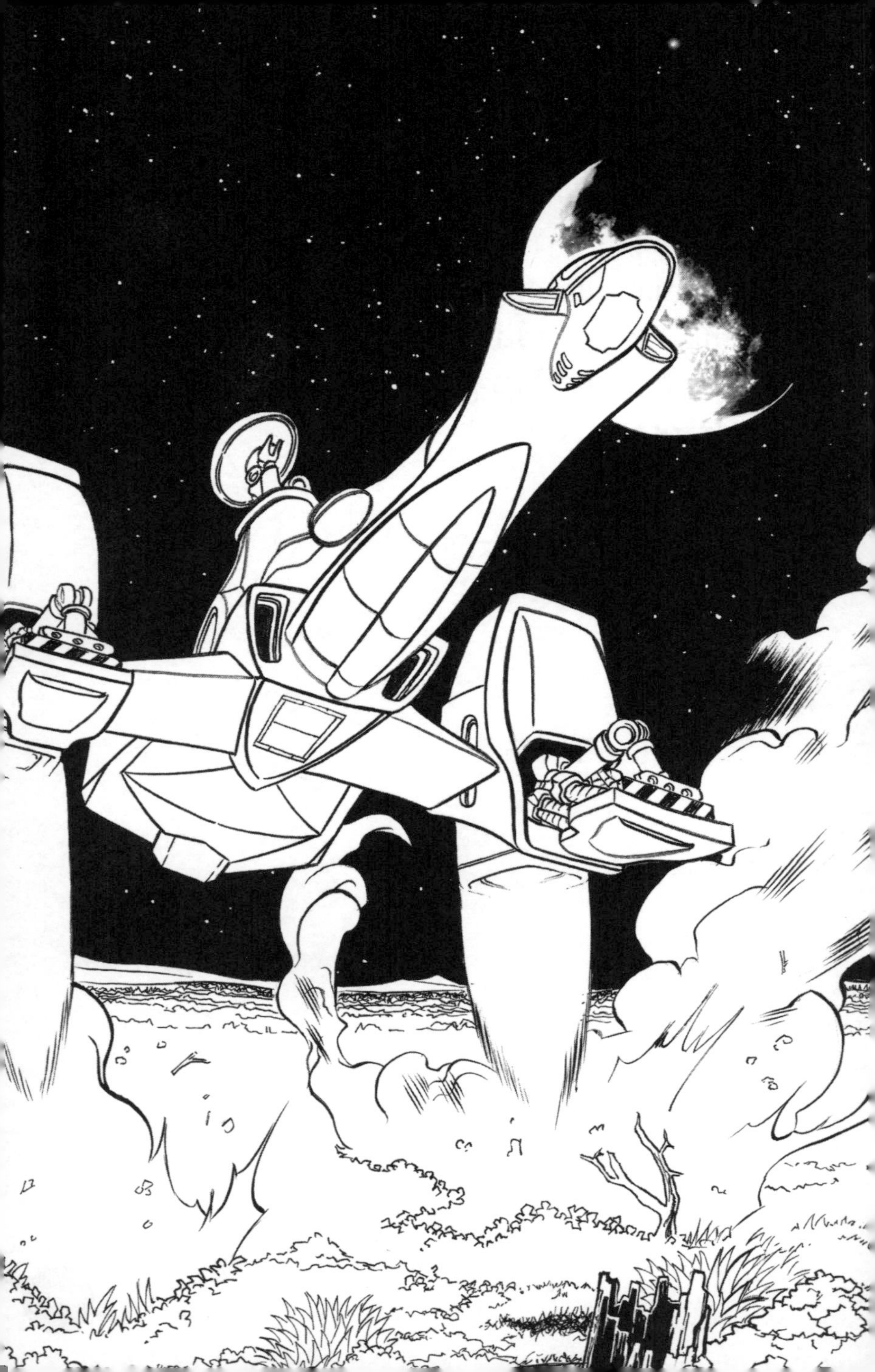

no chance

Suma had done a good job with the laser saw. He had cut four small clear areas in the forest, one for each landing leg.

The Lightspinner dropped slowly from the sky, brilliantly controlled by Finn with his V-helmet.

When the Lightspinner was in just the right position, Finn lowered the landing legs. They touched the ground in the centre of each of the clear spaces.

One of the landing legs had a ladder, and Misha climbed down to meet the other two. She looked at the lander.

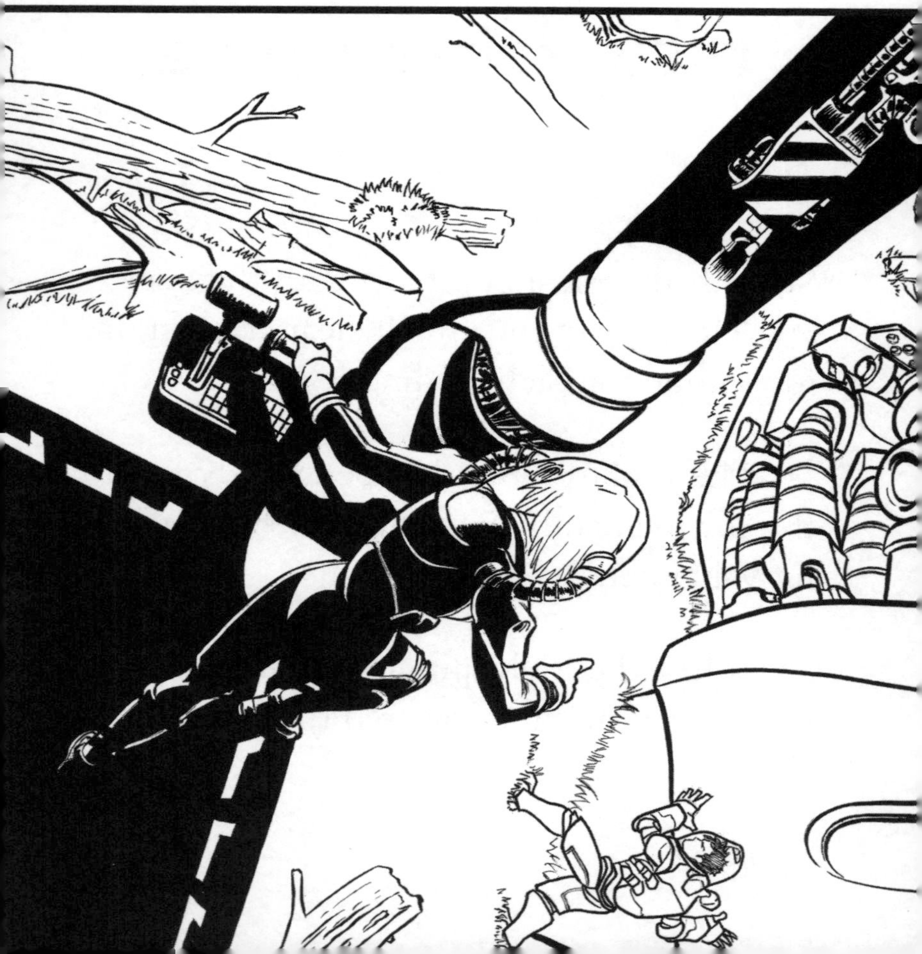

'It's hopeless. As soon as you cut one piece free, another one grows in its place,' Finn said.

The flowers were dying back now. Big, brown seeds were starting to form.

'I've got an idea,' said Suma. 'Let's not take off straight away. Once the plants have produced their seeds, they might stop growing and die back. We might be able to free up the lander.'

'How long do you think we should stay?'

'It's getting dark again now. Let's just give it until the morning.'

Misha agreed. If there was any chance of getting the lander back, they had to take it. So they sat the night out on the Lightspinner, watching the three moons dancing across the glowing sky before they went to sleep.

Suma always slept lightly, and he was awake first. He woke the others.

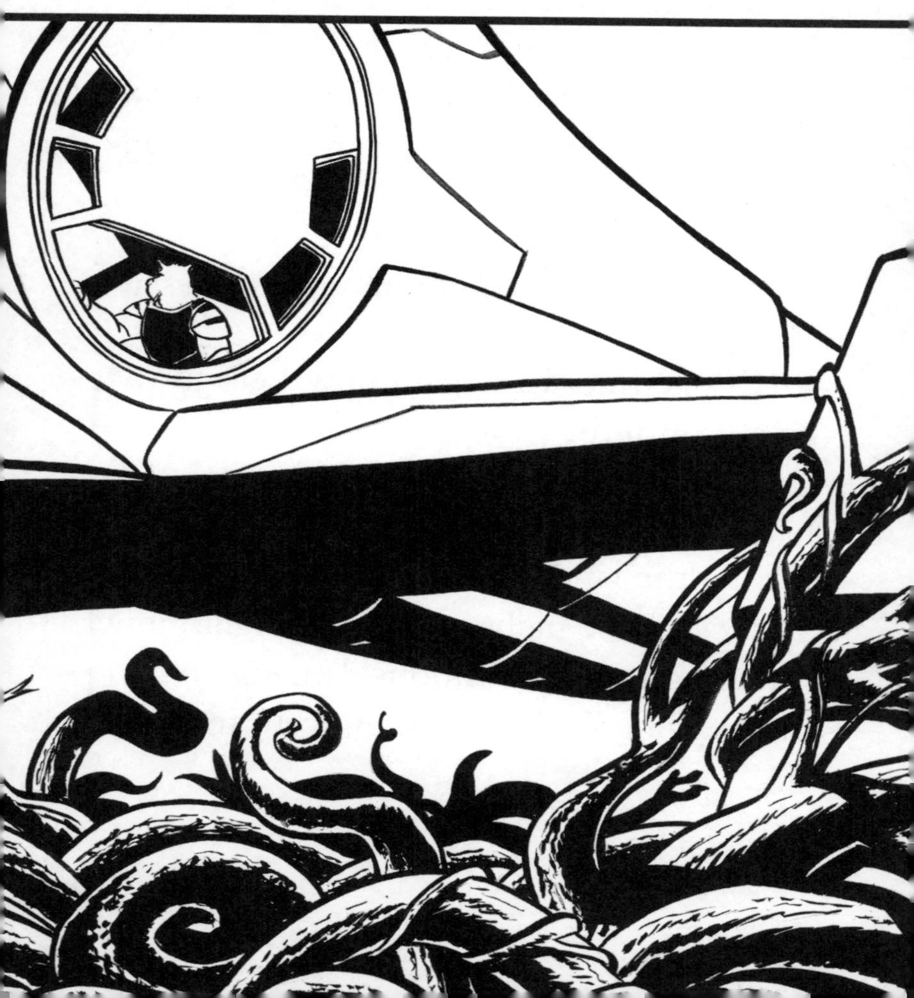

'The creepers! They've grown up in the little clearings I made! They're growing up the landing legs!'

Finn rushed to the pilot's desk. He tried to take off, but the Lightspinner wouldn't move, even under full power. Each landing leg was gripped by a tight net of creepers.

Suma was furious with himself. It had been his idea to stay.

'The seeds of the creepers must be in the ground. As soon as there was a clear space, they started growing!'

And in the depths of the nebula, there was no chance of rescue.

Let's get
out of here!

Finn was watching the scanner screens. He called to the others.

'There's something coming this way. And it's big!'

Suma and Misha looked over Finn's shoulder at the screen.

Bury College
Woodbury LRC

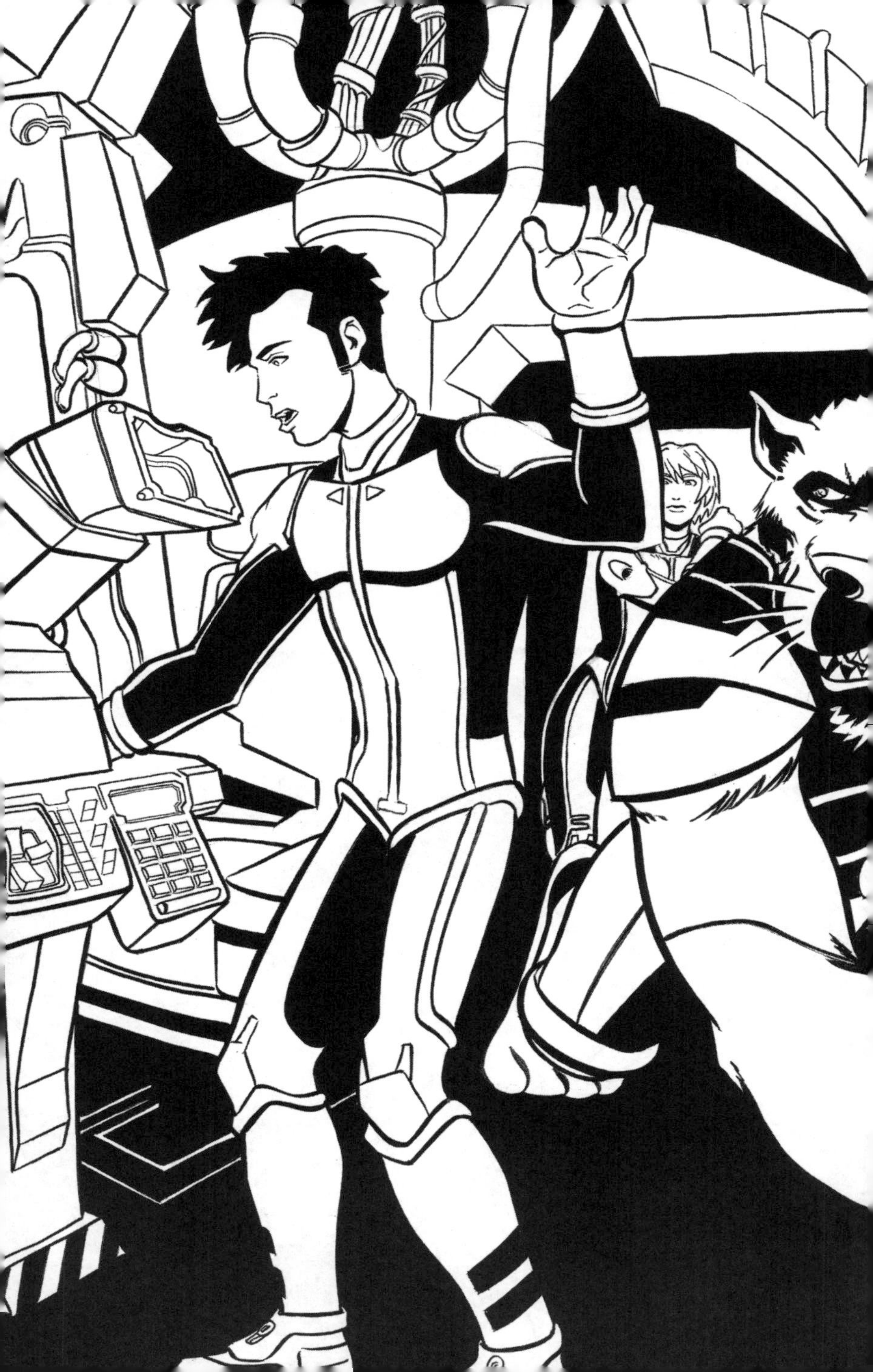

'It's like a great, black cloud, heading towards us! Have you ever seen anything like it, Suma?'

The cloud got closer and closer. And then Suma realised what it was.

'Finn, turn on the sound scanner!'

The screeching noise told them what it was. Birds!

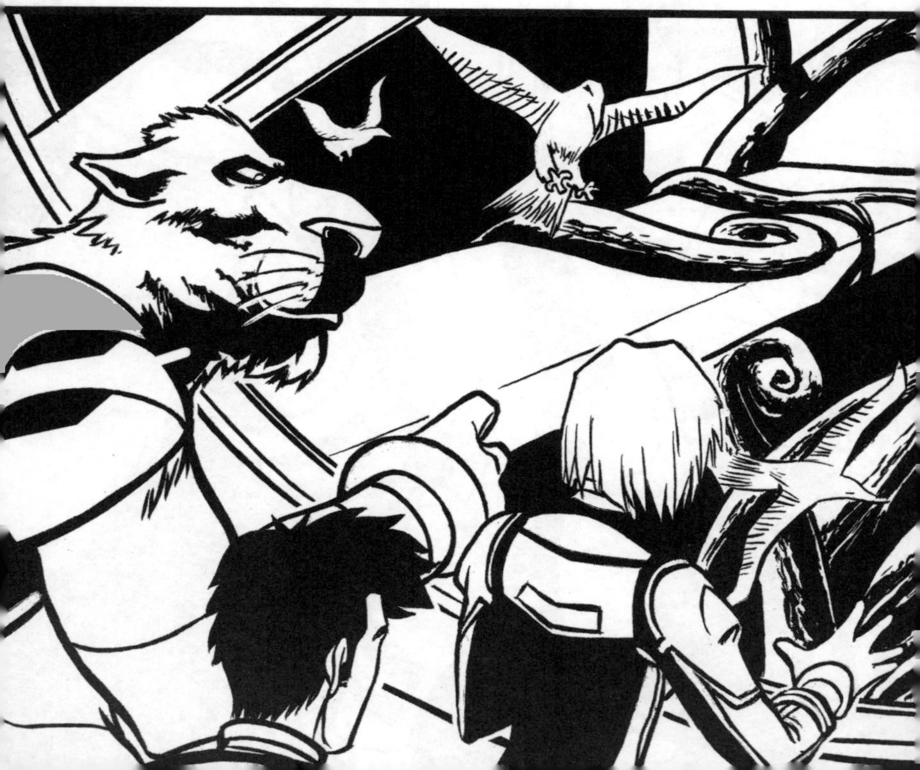

The huge flock swooped down. The Starchasers watched as they started to gobble the brown seeds on the creepers. When all the seeds had gone, they started ripping at the creepers themselves. Soon they were all gone.

'That's why they grow so quickly!' said Suma. 'They need to go through a complete life-cycle before those greedy birds arrive! I guess the birds spread the seeds across the

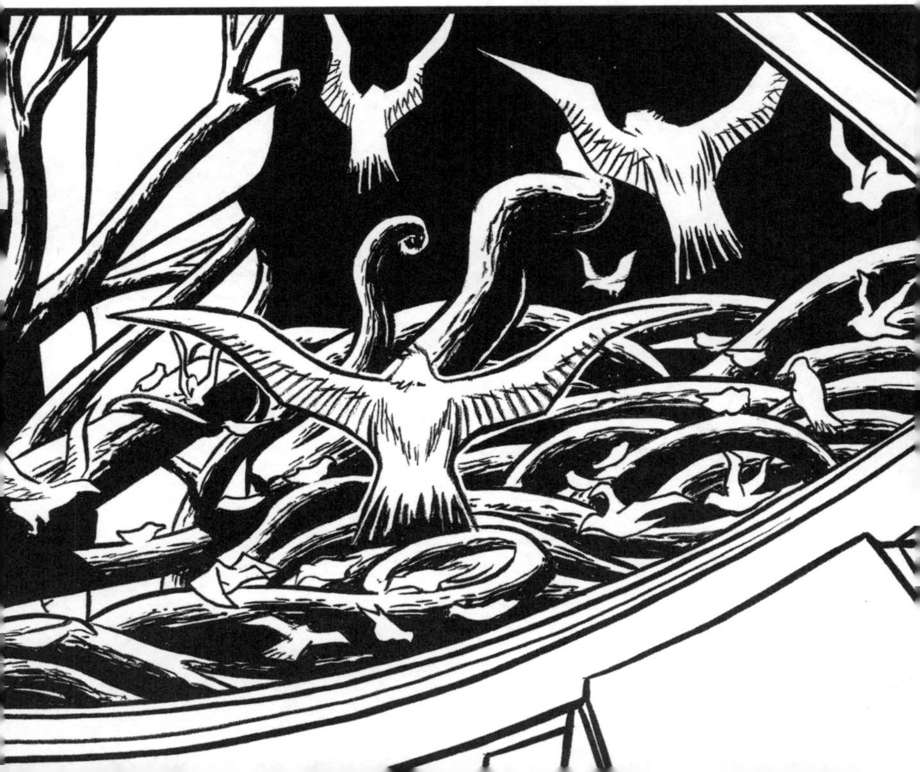

planet in their droppings! Quick! Let's get out of here before it grows back!'

Finn fired up the engines. He could operate the lander by remote control. Flying two ships at once was no problem for Finn!

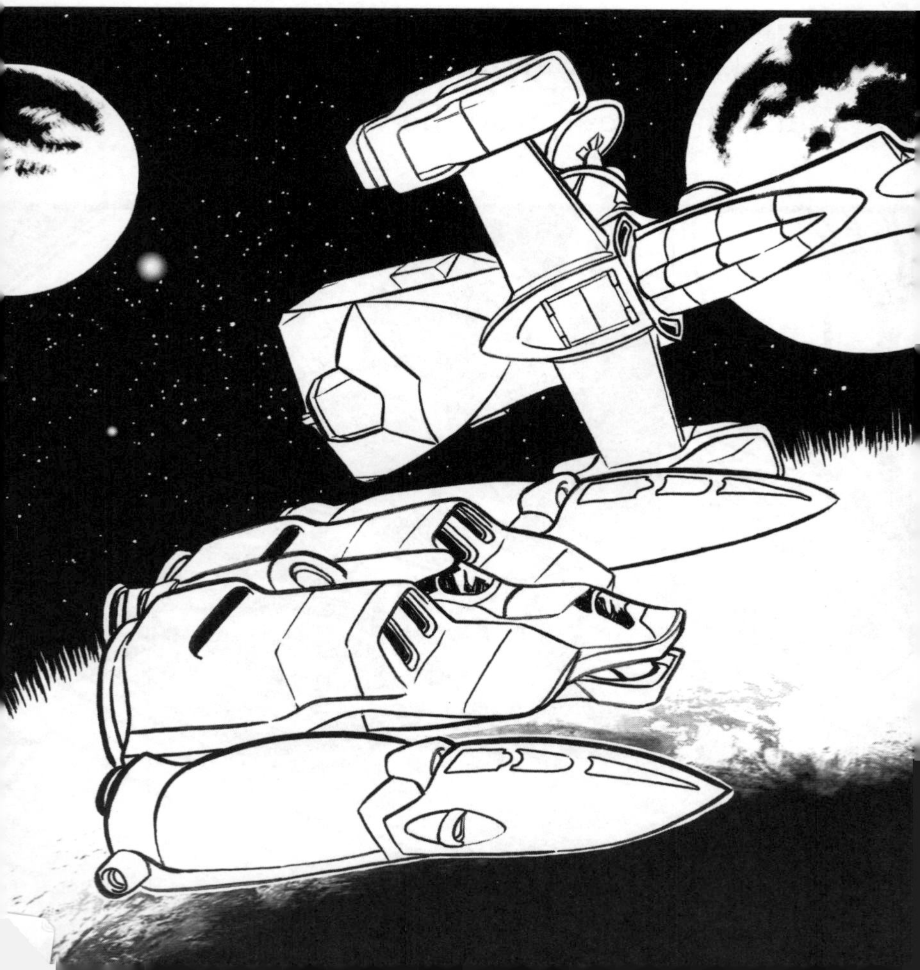

The Starchasers were back on the moonbase.

'What a waste of time!' said Finn. 'I vote we stay out of nebulas in future! We could have been trapped down there for ever!'

'And whose fault would that have been?' snarled Suma. 'What about people who put their friends at risk by playing games when they should have been on watch?'

Finn shut up.

'Anyway, I don't think it was a waste of time.'

He reached into his shoulder bag and brought out three hard, brown seeds.

'Suma, you can't plant that stuff anywhere else. It would take over the planet — unless you took some of those birds as well!'

'Finn, stick to your computer games and leave me to do the science, O.K.? I'm not stupid enough to plant them. They probably wouldn't grow on Earth anyway. But if I look at the way their genes work, and maybe use the fast growing part in other living things, you never know ... '

'You never know what?'

'You might grow up a bit quicker for a start!'